Sports Build Character

CARING IN SPORTS

by Todd Kortemeier

FOCUS READERS

FOCUS READERS

www.focusreaders.com

Copyright © 2018 by Focus Readers, Lake Elmo, MN 55042. All rights reserved. No part of this book may be reproduced or utilized in any form or by any means without written permission from the publisher.

Focus Readers is distributed by North Star Editions:
sales@northstareditions.com | 888-417-0195

Produced for Focus Readers by Red Line Editorial.

Photographs ©: kali9/iStockphoto, cover, 1; FatCamera/iStockphoto, 4–5; Steve Debenport/iStockphoto, 7, 29; Adrian Wyld/The Canadian Press/AP Images, 8–9; Julio Cortez/AP Images, 11; Paul Sancya/AP Images, 12; Chris Pizzello/AP images, 15; Dylan Martinez/Reuters/Newscom, 16; Mike Egerton/PA Wire/URN:28378434/AP Images, 19; Marius Becker/picture-alliance/dpa/AP Images, 20; asiseeit/iStockphoto, 22–23, 26–27; prudkov/iStockphoto, 25

ISBN
978-1-63517-529-5 (hardcover)
978-1-63517-601-8 (paperback)
978-1-63517-745-9 (ebook pdf)
978-1-63517-673-5 (hosted ebook)

Library of Congress Control Number: 2017948109

Printed in the United States of America
Mankato, MN
November, 2017

About the Author

Todd Kortemeier is a writer and editor from Minneapolis. He has written more than 50 books for young people, primarily on sports topics.

TABLE OF CONTENTS

CHAPTER 1
What Is Caring? 5

CHAPTER 2
Caring in Action 9

CHAPTER 3
Caring and You 23

CHARACTER QUESTIONS
Are You Caring? 26

Focus on Caring • 28

Glossary • 30

To Learn More • 31

Index • 32

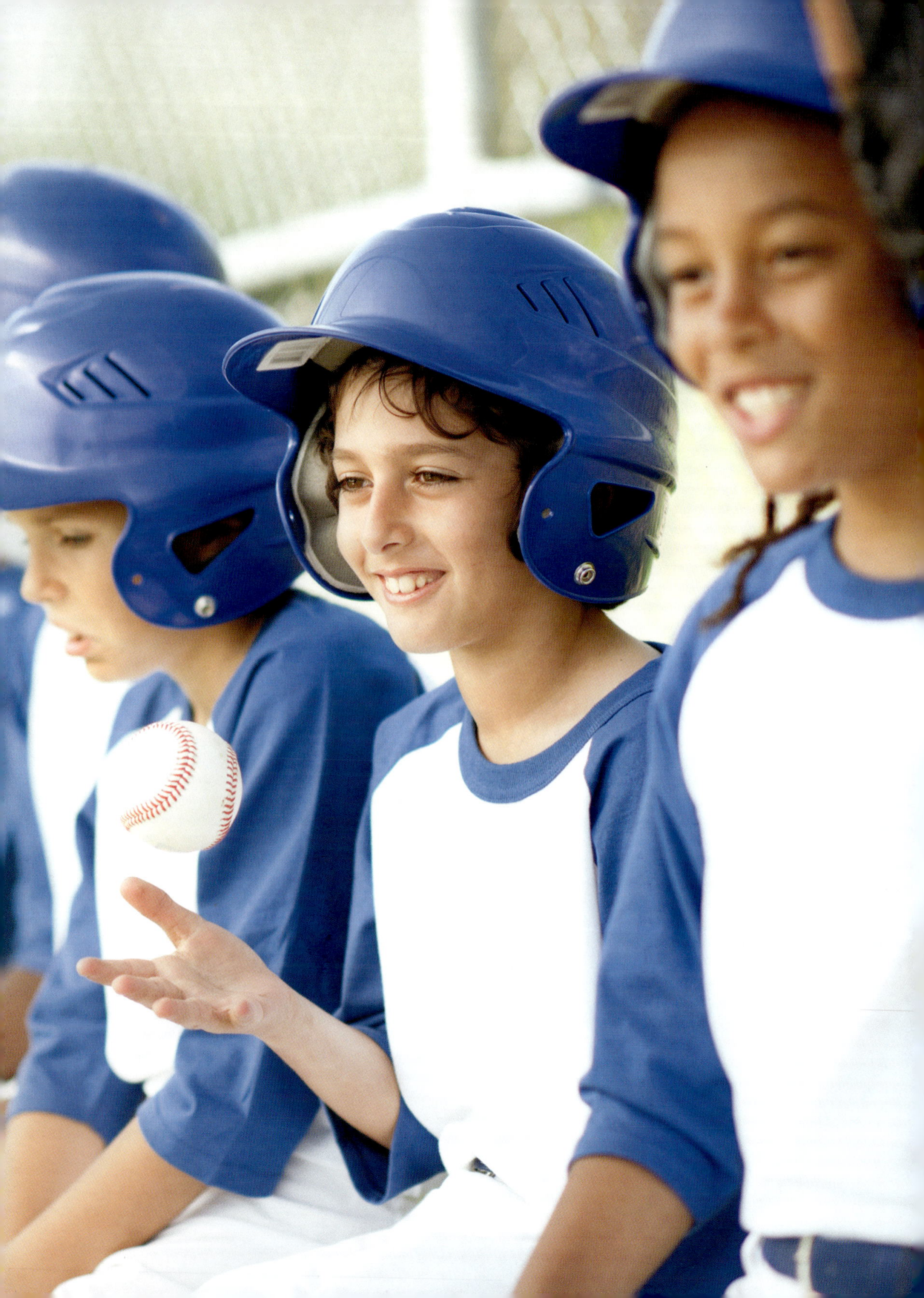

CHAPTER 1

WHAT IS CARING?

Caring means thinking about the feelings of others. It means treating others with kindness. It might not seem like caring is common in sports. After all, sports are about beating the **opponent**.

> **Teammates play better together when they show caring.**

But caring happens often in sports. There are many examples.

Teammates care about one another. They **encourage** and **respect** one another. A coach cares about his or her players, too. Even opponents care about one another. Win or lose, everyone deserves to

LET'S DISCUSS

What are some ways teammates can show that they care about one another?

▷ **Coaches show caring by helping athletes do their best.**

have fun and be safe. All athletes have an interest in that.

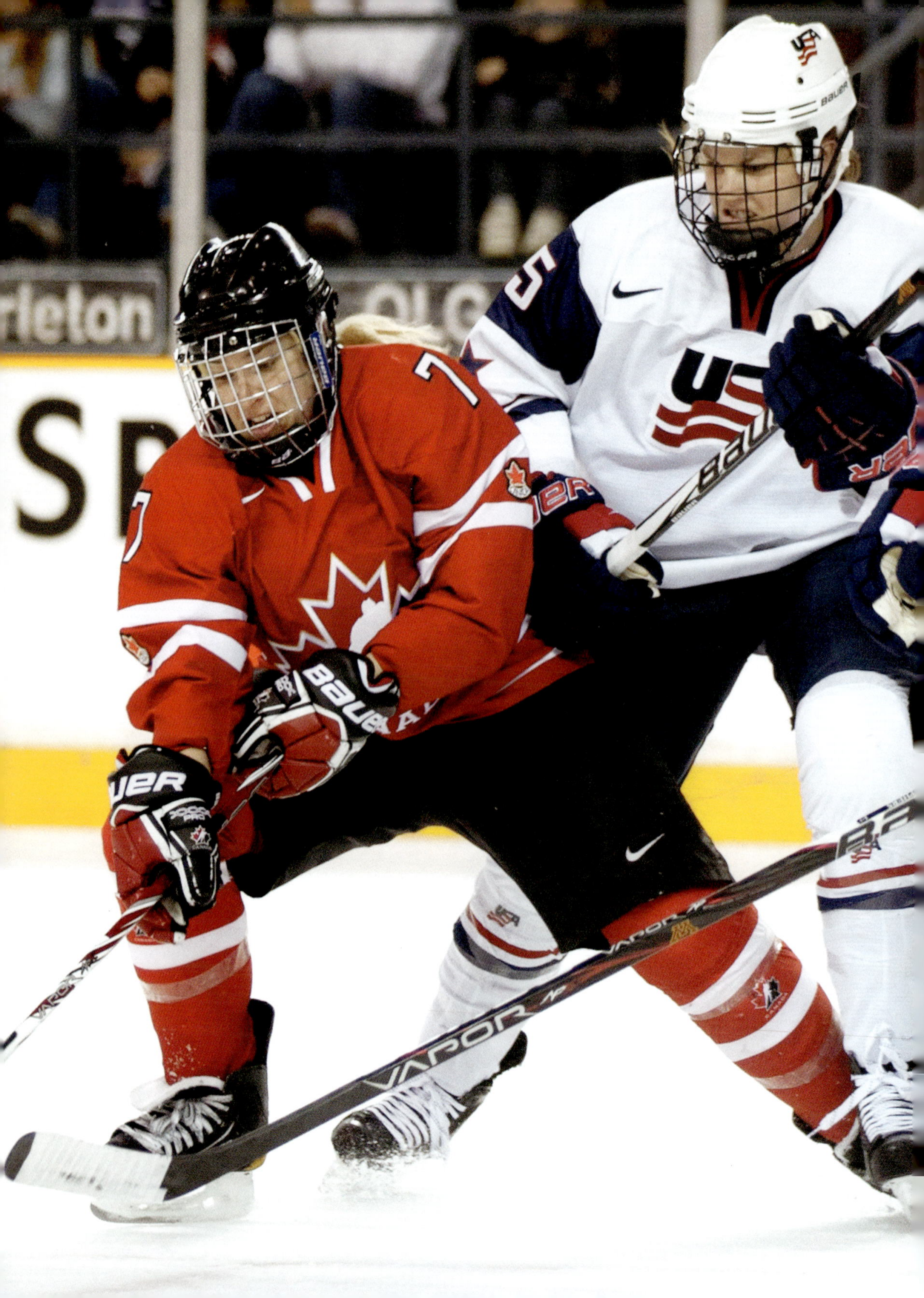
rleton
BAUER
VAPOR

CHAPTER 2

CARING IN ACTION

The United States and Canada are fierce hockey **rivals**. One of the two teams won every women's world championship through 2017. In 2012, the teams opened the **tournament** against each other.

> Opponents on the United States and Canada hockey teams battle for the puck.

Canada forward Haley Irwin got hurt in the first period. She slid into the boards and struggled to stand up. She knew she could not make it back to the bench without help. She asked the closest person for help. It was US goalie Molly Schaus.

The puck was still in play. Schaus had to leave her net open. She

LET'S DISCUSS

What would you do if you saw that a fellow athlete had been injured?

> Irwin (27) has another fall playing against the United States in the 2014 Winter Olympics.

risked letting in a goal. But she skated over to Irwin and gave her a helpful push. Irwin was able to glide to the bench safely. Schaus didn't have to help Irwin. It was a caring thing to do in the heat of battle.

11

▷ **Gallaraga was a good sport after Joyce called the runner safe.**

One of the hardest things to do in baseball is pitch a perfect game. It means not allowing a single batter to reach base. Detroit Tigers pitcher Armando Gallaraga came very close in 2010.

Gallaraga needed just one more out. There was a close play at first base. The throw beat the runner. But **umpire** Jim Joyce called the runner safe. Gallaraga's perfect game was over.

Joyce felt terrible when he learned that he had made the wrong call. Umpires usually stand by the calls they make. But Joyce told Gallaraga he was sorry. Gallaraga was not angry. Instead he said, "Nobody's perfect."

The next day, the Tigers honored Gallaraga before the game. The umpire and player shook hands. Gallaraga showed there were no hard feelings.

Tigers fans were mad. But they respected Joyce for admitting his mistake. And they saw Gallaraga's

LET'S DISCUSS

Athletes learn perseverance through **practice**. What other things can you learn by playing sports?

> **Joyce (left) and Gallaraga shake hands at an awards ceremony.**

example. He chose to forgive Joyce. The fans stood and cheered. Both men showed kindness and caring in a tough situation.

15

▷ **D'Agostino (left) accepts help from her opponent.**

The Olympic Games take place every few years. Athletes work their whole lives to make it there. Just being there is a huge achievement.

16

Runners Abbey D'Agostino and Nikki Hamblin were both first-time Olympians in 2016. D'Agostino was American, and Hamblin was from New Zealand. They were competing in the 5,000-meter race.

With about 2,000 meters left in the race, the two runners collided.

LET'S DISCUSS

Imagine that you are a coach. Would you want a player on your team who is very talented but not caring?

Hamblin had slowed down, and D'Agostino ran into her. The collision knocked both of them to the ground. D'Agostino got up first. But she saw Hamblin was still down in pain. She stopped to help her up.

D'Agostino also was hurt. An ankle **injury** meant she couldn't run at her normal pace. Hamblin slowed down to stay with her. The runners encouraged each other the rest of the way. Both of them finished the race. They later received the Fair

> Hamblin and two helpers assist D'Agostino into a wheelchair after the race.

Play Award. The award recognizes sportsmanship and kindness in competition.

19

Brazil's David Luiz (4) puts his arm around a disappointed Rodriguez.

Every soccer player dreams of winning the World Cup. In 2014, James Rodriguez was one of the best players in the tournament. The Colombian led all players with six goals. And he led his team to the

quarterfinals. There they faced mighty Brazil. Down 2–0, Rodriguez scored to make it 2–1. But Colombia couldn't get another goal. They lost and were out of the tournament.

Rodriguez was in tears. Brazil's David Luiz went over to **comfort** him. Luiz also encouraged the crowd to cheer for Rodriguez. Even though the crowd was mostly Brazil fans, they showed their respect. Luiz's kindness helped Rodriguez handle the loss.

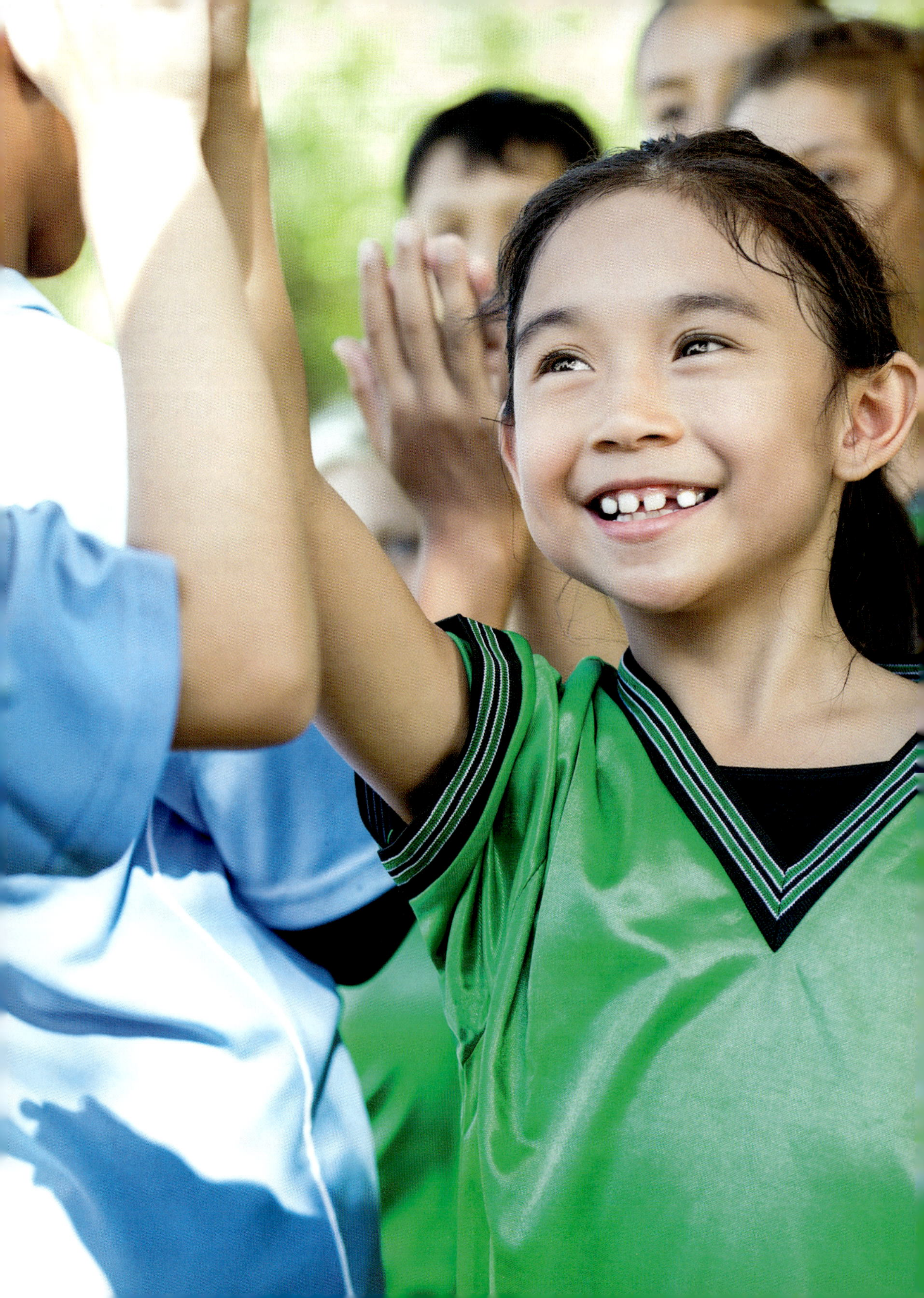

CHAPTER 3

CARING AND YOU

Caring is an important part of sports. Fair play and sportsmanship are basic values. Caring is a key part of both. It might not always be easy.

> **Shaking hands after a game is a great way to show caring for your opponent.**

An athlete's mind might be on other things.

Caring doesn't stop when the game ends. You, your teammates, coaches, and opponents are all in this together. Everyone plays a part. Caring can take many forms. It could be showing understanding when someone makes a mistake.

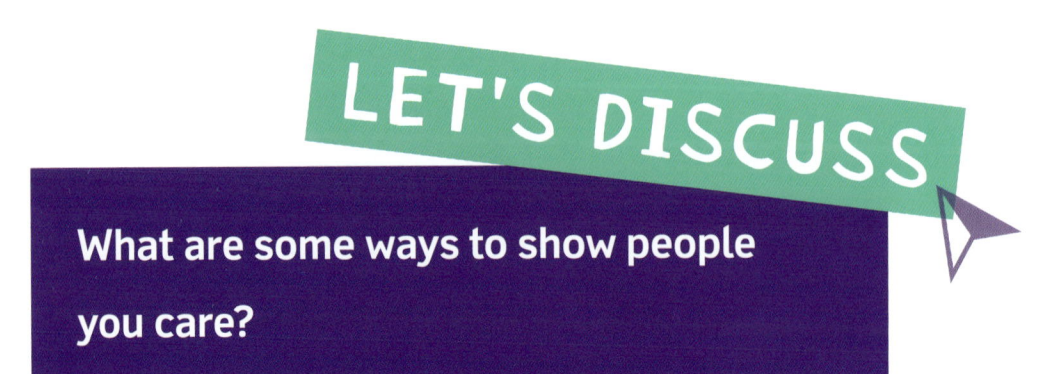

LET'S DISCUSS

What are some ways to show people you care?

▷ **You can show caring when a friend is having a bad day.**

Or it could be treating a teammate with kindness. Caring is simple. But it can make a big difference.

CHARACTER QUESTIONS

ARE YOU CARING?

Ask yourself these questions and decide.
- Do I notice how others are feeling?
- Am I ever mean to people on purpose?
- Am I usually kind and nice to people?
- Do I try to help others when I can?
- Do my friends know I care about them?

It's never too late to be more caring! Challenge yourself today to do one kind act. You could ask a friend how he or she is feeling. You could also offer to do an extra chore at home.

Spending time with someone is one way to show you care.

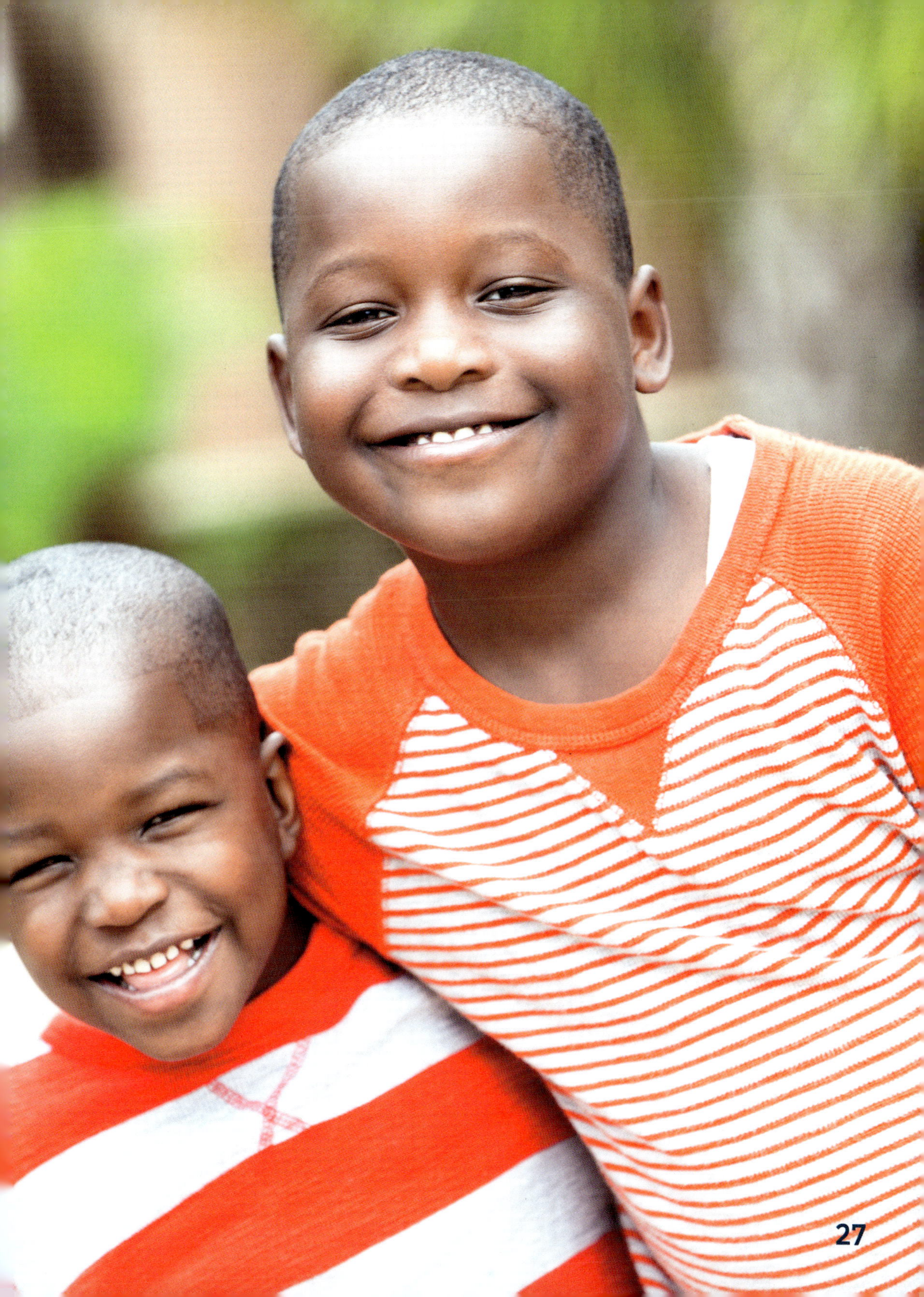

FOCUS ON
CARING

Write your answers on a separate piece of paper.

1. Write a summary of how each person showed caring in Chapter 2.

2. Explain how you would have reacted if you were Armando Gallaraga.

3. What award did Abbey D'Agostino and Nikki Hamblin receive from the Olympics?
    - A. the Good Sport Award
    - B. the Fair Play Award
    - C. the Gold Medal

4. Suppose Armando Gallaraga had allowed a walk instead of a hit. Would it have been a perfect game?
    - A. Yes, because he didn't allow a hit.
    - B. No, because a walk counts as a base hit.
    - C. No, because a perfect game means not allowing any runners on base.

5. What does **race** mean in this book?

*D'Agostino was American, and Hamblin was from New Zealand. They were competing in the 5,000-meter **race**.*

    A. a running contest
    B. the color of a person's skin
    C. an athletic field

6. What does **called** mean in this book?

*The throw beat the runner. But umpire Jim Joyce **called** the runner safe.*

    A. decided a play
    B. talked on the phone
    C. had a fun time

Answer key on page 32.

GLOSSARY

comfort
To help someone feel better.

encourage
To urge someone to do well.

injury
Specific harm done to a person.

opponent
The other person or team in a competition.

practice
To work on skills outside of competition.

quarterfinals
The third-to-last round of a competition.

respect
To treat others with care for their feelings and happiness.

rivals
Teams or players that have an intense and ongoing competition against one another.

tournament
A competition that includes many teams.

umpire
A person on the baseball field who is in charge of the rules.

TO LEARN MORE

BOOKS

Martineau, Susan. *Caring for Others*. Mankato, MN: Smart Apple Media, 2012.

Nelson, Robin. *How Can I Help? A Book About Caring*. Minneapolis: Lerner Publications, 2014.

Raatma, Lucia. *Caring*. Ann Arbor, MI: Cherry Lake Publishing, 2014.

NOTE TO EDUCATORS

Visit **www.focusreaders.com** to find lesson plans, activities, links, and other resources related to this title.

INDEX

B
Brazil, 21

C
Canada, 9–10
Colombia, 20–21

D
D'Agostino, Abbey, 17–18
Detroit Tigers, 12, 14

F
Fair Play Award, 18–19

G
Gallaraga, Armando, 12–15

H
Hamblin, Nikki, 17–18

I
Irwin, Haley, 10–11

J
Joyce, Jim, 13–15

L
Luiz, David, 21

N
New Zealand, 17

O
Olympic Games, 16

R
Rodriguez, James, 20–21

S
Schaus, Molly, 10–11

U
United States, 9

Answer Key: 1. Answers will vary; **2.** Answers will vary; **3.** B; **4.** C; **5.** A; **6.** A